BIG APPLE BARN™

HAPPY GO LUCKY

by **KRISTIN EARHART**

Illustrations by
JOHN STEVEN GURNEY

A
LITTLE APPLE
PAPERBACK

SCHOLASTIC INC.
New York   Toronto   London   Auckland   Sydney
Mexico City   New Delhi   Hong Kong   Buenos Aires

*To my mom, who inspired me with her love of horses —
and so much more.*

*And my dad, who never flinched when I said, "I want a
pony," and not even when I claimed, "Now I need a horse."*

With lots of love and gratitude.   —K.J.E.

No part of this publication may be reproduced, stored in a retrieval system,
or transmitted in any form or by any means, electronic, mechanical,
photocopying, recording, or otherwise, without written permission of
the publisher. For information regarding permission, write to Scholastic Inc.,
Attention: Permissions Department, 557 Broadway, New York, NY 10012.

ISBN-13: 978-0-439-89371-8
ISBN-10: 0-439-89371-2

Text copyright © 2006 by Kristin Earhart.
Illustrations copyright © 2006 by Scholastic Inc.
SCHOLASTIC, LITTLE APPLE, BIG APPLE BARN, and associated logos
are trademarks and/or registered trademarks of Scholastic Inc.

12 11 10 9 8 7 6 5 4   7 8 9 10 11/0
                                              40

Printed in the U.S.A.
First printing, September 2006

Contents

Chapter One

The Good Life

The sun was bright and high in the sky. Happy could not have been happier as he looked out of his stall. It was the perfect day for eating fresh, green grass. The big field behind his barn was full of the tasty stuff, and Happy could walk out of his stall and into the pasture whenever he wanted. The grass was delicious, and the patches of clover were sweet. Life was good.

Happy shook the straw from his coat and walked to his stall door.

"Happy! Happy Go Lucky!"

Happy knew the voice at once. It was Mrs. Shoemaker. She was the owner of Shoemaker Stables. She took care of Happy and his mom.

"Happy Go Lucky!"

Mrs. Shoemaker had called him by his full name, so Happy knew something exciting was about to happen. Mrs. Shoemaker only used his full name for special occasions. Happy Go Lucky trotted out of the barn with a snort and headed toward the pasture gate. Mrs. Shoemaker always waited for him there. Happy gave a little buck to show off for her. She always laughed when he did that. But when he got to the gate, Mrs. Shoemaker was not laughing. And she was not alone.

"Oh, Happy," Mrs. Shoemaker said with a sigh. Then she smiled.

Happy loved the sound of Mrs. Shoemaker's voice. It was as tender as the first grass that grows after winter — and so was her touch. Mrs. Shoemaker reached out to smooth Happy's coat.

"Happy Go Lucky," Mrs. Shoemaker said, "I would like you to meet Diane. Diane knows a lot about ponies." She nodded to the woman standing next to her.

Happy looked at the new woman. Diane. *She may think she knows a lot about ponies,* Happy thought. *But I am a pony. Who knows more about ponies than an actual pony?*

Still, Happy was curious. He looked at Diane carefully. She was much taller than Mrs. Shoemaker.

"Hello, Happy!" Diane said.

Do you have to talk so loud? Happy thought. *I'm right here.* Mrs. Shoemaker never talked like that.

Diane reached out and gave him a firm pat. Happy was surprised at first, but then he relaxed. This Diane obviously knew that ponies like a hearty pat on the shoulder.

"He's pretty young," Diane said. Her voice was softer now. Happy pricked his ears

forward to hear her. "He is a good size, though," Diane went on.

"And he is wonderfully sweet," Mrs. Shoemaker added.

Sure enough, Happy thought, standing up straight. *They're talking about me.*

"He looks healthy, too. I have never seen such a shiny coat."

Happy had to agree with Diane. His brown coat had a reddish glow. And Mrs. Shoemaker always said his black mane and tail were silky soft.

Just then, Happy's mom walked up next to him. Happy turned his head and nickered.

"Hello, Gracie," Mrs. Shoemaker and Diane said at the same time.

Happy knew that Gracie was his mom's name. Diane seemed to know that, too. Happy tilted his head to one side. *Does Diane know my mom?*

Gracie touched Happy's nose with her own. She always nuzzled him that way in the morning. Then, she trotted into the field toward their favorite patch of clover.

Happy couldn't resist. He loved getting attention from Mrs. Shoemaker, but he also loved that clover. He spun around and cantered off behind Gracie. She was a little taller than Happy, but she was still short enough to be a pony and not a horse. They stopped at the edge of the clover patch and started to eat.

"Hey, they were talking about me," Happy said as he took a big bite of clover.

"Happy, dear. You know better than to talk with your mouth full," his mom told him. "Son, you must remember these things. Someday I will not be around to remind you."

"What?" Happy asked. He was still chewing a long piece of clover with a pink flower on the end. The flowers tickled a little, but they tasted like sugar. "What do you mean?" His mom lived in the stall right next to him. Happy could see her whenever he wanted.

"Happy, you've grown up," his mom said. "You're not a colt anymore."

There was something different in Gracie's voice. She sounded sad, but she was smiling.

"Son," she continued. "It is time for you to go to a new home. You've learned all that I can teach you."

A new home? This was news to Happy.

Happy's mom tried to explain everything

to him, but Happy didn't understand. He needed to go to a new place with other ponies? He still had a lot to learn? Happy was confused. He knew he was a big pony now. He was proud of that, but he wasn't ready for everything else to change.

Chapter Two

A School Pony

Happy couldn't believe it. Mrs. Shoemaker was going to sell him to Diane — Diane, who knew a lot about ponies. Happy's mom said that Diane was a teacher.

"You must understand that Diane's work is important, Happy," Gracie explained. "It is her job to teach children how to ride ponies, and she teaches ponies to be good when children ride them. It is not an easy job."

Happy wasn't sure what his mom was

saying. He already knew how to wear a saddle and bridle. He could walk, trot, canter, and stop. What else could Diane teach him?

"A good pony is many things," Gracie said. "A good pony isn't just good with one rider. A really good pony can be ridden by many different people."

"But I am good for Mrs. Shoemaker," Happy complained. Mrs. Shoemaker was the person who had taught Happy to wear a saddle and let someone sit on him. "I don't need to know how to carry anybody else!" Happy stamped his hoof on the ground.

Gracie gave her son a long look. "Dear, you know that won't do. You need to understand that a pony does not just carry his rider," she said. "A pony and his rider work together."

"I know, I know," Happy grumbled softly, swishing his tail. "But I work just fine with

Mrs. Shoemaker. I don't see why I have to carry anyone else. And I definitely don't see why I have to live somewhere else."

Happy snorted and trotted away from Gracie. He liked living with Mrs. Shoemaker. He liked his grassy green field. And he especially liked being close to his mom. But not right now. Right now, he wanted to be as far away from her as possible.

His mom just didn't understand. She said that he should go away with Diane. She said that it would be best for him. "How does she know what's best for me?" Happy asked himself, kicking at a crab apple. "I want to stay here. Shoemaker Stables is the best place for a pony."

He walked around the field, dragging his hooves. Shoemaker Stables really was a great home. Mrs. Shoemaker gave him carrots and apples. He could go out into the pasture whenever he wanted, and eat the tastiest grass and clover.

But he wasn't hungry for grass. He didn't even want clover. A bright yellow butterfly flapped by his nose, and Happy didn't bother to chase it.

"Oh, Happy Go Lucky!" Mrs. Shoemaker called.

Happy pricked his ears. Mrs. Shoemaker sounded glad. *Maybe I'm not leaving after all,* Happy thought. He sprang into a bouncy jog and headed for the fence.

"Happy, I am very proud of you," Mrs. Shoemaker said. "As of tomorrow, you will be a school pony!"

Tomorrow? Happy thought, surprised. *A school pony!* His head drooped.

Mrs. Shoemaker patted him for a long time. "It's such wonderful news. We should celebrate," she said, reaching into her pocket and pulling out an apple. But Happy didn't feel like celebrating. He stepped away from the fence, and ran all the way to the barn.

When he reached his stall, Happy lay down. He snuggled his nose against his side like he had done when he was just a colt. He breathed in the smell of the sweet straw.

Then Gracie's head appeared over the stall wall. "Happy, dear," she said. "Please know I wish you could stay. But the time has come for you to leave. You have so much to offer. Mrs. Shoemaker believes you will be a wonderful school pony. I must say, I do, too." Gracie paused. "That doesn't mean I won't miss you. I will. More than you know."

Happy didn't want to listen. But his mom's words were warm. Her voice was kind. He trusted her.

"Many children will learn to ride with you, my son," Gracie said. "Being a school pony is an important job. Mrs. Shoemaker knows this. I do, too."

Happy raised his head and looked at his mom. Then he looked out at the field. Beyond the crab-apple tree, he could see Mrs. Shoemaker walking toward her house. He couldn't believe that tomorrow he would have to say good-bye.

He sighed as he remembered the first time he had stepped to the door of the little barn on his wobbly legs. That was when he was just a foal. Happy had been curious and a little afraid. But his mom had nudged him with her soft nose. When Happy had finally walked out into the field, Mrs. Shoemaker had clapped and said the most encouraging things.

The world had seemed so big on that spring morning, so bright. The sun had been warm on his back. There had been lots of new smells! All of those smells were familiar now.

Tomorrow would bring many more new things — some of the first new things Happy had experienced in a long time. Would they ever feel familiar? Happy sighed. He could hear his mom in the stall next door. He had so many questions, but he was tired now. His questions would have to wait until tomorrow.

Chapter Three

Saying Good-bye

Happy awoke to the friendly chatter of the birds who lived in the barn. Everything seemed the same, until he remembered that this was his last day at Shoemaker Stables. Happy pushed himself onto his legs. He usually slept standing up, but he had been so tired from all the news that he had slept the whole night on the ground.

His mom's stall was still quiet, so he

headed out into the field alone. He had to hurry! There was a lot to do before he left.

First on his list was a quick visit to the crab-apple tree. The fruit was too sour to eat, but Happy loved the crooked old tree. It had one branch that was perfect for scratching his back. No morning was complete without a trip to the crab-apple tree.

Second, he trotted along the edge of the pasture fence to the far field. From there he could see his favorite part of the farm. The lush valley was misty in the morning chill. Happy leaned against the top rail of the fence and took a deep breath. He wanted to always remember this. The valley was so beautiful and it seemed to go on forever. He knew there could be nothing like it anywhere else, and he would probably never see it again. He didn't want to leave the far field, but he knew he didn't have much time. With a sigh, Happy continued along the fence.

He planned on making several trips to the clover patch before he had to leave, and he would make his first now. He trotted to the center of the pasture and dug his nose deep in the sweetness. He closed his eyes and chewed, trying to taste every clover leaf.

"You will find clover at your new home, I promise."

Happy raised his head at the sound of the familiar voice. His mother stood next to him.

"How do you know?" Happy asked.

"I simply do," she answered.

Now that Happy had asked one question, he had a hundred more. His mother seemed so certain that this new home was a good place. Happy needed to know why. Just as he was about to ask, a clatter rang over the yard.

A fancy truck and trailer rumbled down the farm's tiny dirt road. As it came closer, Happy could see that Diane was the driver.

No! Not yet! Happy had so much more to do! He needed to say a proper good-bye to everyone, to everything. He saw Mrs. Shoemaker rush from her house, still in her robe. Happy's eyes flashed to his mom's. He thought he would see comfort there, but she, too, was alarmed.

"Happy, dear," she began. "I didn't think Diane would come so early."

Happy's eyes darted from his mom to the fancy trailer and back to his mom. "What can we do?" he asked. "We have to do something! I'm not ready yet!" Happy spun in a circle and thought about where he should hide. He could jump the fence in the far field. It wasn't very high, and the top rail was loose where he always leaned against it. That was it! That was his plan.

"Son," Happy's mother said. "You are ready. You are more than ready." Gracie stepped toward him and rested her head over her son's neck.

Happy thought again about the fence in the back field. If he jumped it, he could run into the valley. Diane would leave without him, and then he could stay with his mom

forever. But at that moment, he felt Gracie's warm breath against his cheek, and he could not leave her side.

"Happy." Gracie's voice was soft and warm. "I am certain of one thing," she said, nuzzling his neck. "You will make me proud."

Happy lifted his nose to hers, and they touched.

Just then, he heard Mrs. Shoemaker. "Well, I didn't even get a chance to brush him. I had wanted him to look his best for you."

"Oh, he doesn't need to be clean for the trailer," Diane said quickly. "Let's get him wrapped up and ready to go. It will be great to get him to my place before lunchtime. My daughters are excited to meet him."

Happy didn't budge from his mother's side. Mrs. Shoemaker had to come into the field to get him. Happy reached his muzzle out toward Gracie again, and she playfully nibbled his mane. "We'll see each other again," she whispered.

Then, Mrs. Shoemaker gave his halter a tug. "Come on, Happy," she said. "It's time."

Mrs. Shoemaker held his halter and rubbed behind his ears as Diane ran the cloth wraps around his legs.

"These will keep you safe for your ride," Mrs. Shoemaker explained. "The padding will protect your legs, so you don't bump yourself and get hurt."

"All set," Diane announced. "Let's load him in the trailer."

"Let me lead him in," Mrs. Shoemaker said, her voice unsteady. "He's new at this."

As Happy stepped forward, he felt funny. He lifted his legs high, trying to shake off the wraps. "It's okay, Happy," Mrs. Shoemaker said. "You'll get used to them." Happy wasn't so sure, but he followed Mrs. Shoemaker into the trailer. Before he knew it, the back door was closed behind him. At least Mrs. Shoemaker was still there.

"Oh, Happy." She sighed. "You have been such a good boy and so much fun. I know you'll do great things. I will never forget you." She bent down and gave his muzzle a kiss.

Happy didn't know how to say good-bye, so he nibbled her hair — just like his mom had nibbled his mane. Mrs. Shoemaker laughed. "You always were a rascal," she said. Then she patted his neck and stepped out the side door.

The truck roared to life again, and Happy could hear traces of voices drowned out by the sound. He stepped forward and looked out the window. The trailer began to rattle, and Happy could tell he was moving.

He reached his neck out the window. His mom and Mrs. Shoemaker stood side by side at the fence. He whinnied. Gracie whinnied back, tossing her head up and down as Mrs. Shoemaker waved. Happy could see them getting smaller and smaller. He stretched his neck out farther. As the truck and trailer rounded the bend, he could still see them. Still, still, still . . . and then they were gone.

Chapter Four

A New Home

All alone in the trailer, Happy tried to figure out where Diane was taking him. He watched the trees zoom by. He kept an eye out for anything that looked familiar. But everything was new, and once the truck pulled onto a wide, smooth road, Happy realized he would never find his way back to Shoemaker Stables. Everything was passing too quickly.

Happy tried to eat some hay to keep his mind off all of the changes. The hay tasted dry, but he ate it anyway. It smelled better than the bitter, burnt air from the road. Happy tried to remember what his paddock smelled like on a spring morning. That memory came back easily, and then a dozen more came with it. He missed his old home already.

Happy was surprised when he heard the truck's rumble slow down. The truck stopped, and he noticed that the air suddenly tasted fresher. He heard a slam, and then Diane's face appeared in the trailer window.

"Well, this is it, Happy," Diane said. Her voice was bright, and she gave Happy a quick smile. "Welcome to Big Apple Barn. I hope you like it here."

Happy watched as Diane headed to the back of the trailer. *Big Apple Barn,* he thought. *That sounds kind of nice. I like*

apples, and the big ones are always sweet. It's a good name. Maybe this place won't be so bad, after all.

The trailer door swung open, and Diane appeared with a lead rope. The next thing Happy knew, he was backing out of the trailer.

Happy took a deep breath and looked around. On one side, there was a white house with a short white fence. Next, Happy spotted a tall tree with a swing. But then Diane led him in the other direction. That's when Happy saw the big red barn. It was huge! How had he not seen it before? Diane gave the rope a light tug, and Happy followed her through the wide barn doors.

This barn was nothing like Happy's simple stable back at Mrs. Shoemaker's. There was a hard, even floor under his hooves. Horses stood in wooden stalls on

both sides of the walkway. Each stall had a
window with thin bars over it, so the horses
could see out. As Happy followed Diane up
the long path, the horses came to the front
of their stalls to look at him.

Happy had never seen so many horses!
His mother had told him about horses that
roamed together in the wild. And she
had talked about how some horses lived
together in large barns, each in a box with

walls on all sides. But Happy never thought he'd see such a place for himself. His stable at Mrs. Shoemaker's had been open to the pasture, and the wall between his and his mom's space had been short enough that they could lean over it and talk. Happy had loved that.

But Happy didn't mind the high walls in these stalls. Looking at all of the different horses, Happy could tell he wouldn't know what to say to them. These horses were all tall and noble, and Happy was not sure what they were thinking as they gazed down at him. Some of them snorted and looked away, but none of them said a word.

As Diane led him down the aisle, Happy noticed that there were some other ponies in the barn, too. They were also watching as Happy walked by. Happy thought the other ponies looked older than him. He tried to hold his head up and lift his hooves high, but he still felt very young and very new.

"Here we are," Diane announced. "Your very own home." She slid open the bolt on a wooden door and unclipped the rope from Happy's halter. Then she pointed him into the dark stall. Happy stopped cold. He snorted and his ears twitched. He couldn't go in there. It was pitch-black!

"Go on," Diane encouraged.

Happy looked at Diane and then back into the stall. All at once, Diane gave him a firm pat on his hindquarters. Happy skidded forward. He turned around as fast as he could, but Diane had already closed the door. He was trapped.

He stepped toward the stall window, wanting to look out. But then he heard a loud slamming sound, followed by pounding footsteps. Happy bolted back into the darkness of the stall, trembling.

"Is he here, Mom? Can we see him?" begged a young girl's voice.

"Ivy, quiet please," Diane said. "You know not to yell in the barn."

"Did you pick up the new school pony, Mom?" another voice asked.

"Yes, Andrea," Diane answered. "But he's still very nervous. This is all new to him. You and your sister can look at him, but please don't go in the stall yet."

Almost immediately, Happy saw two faces appear at the stall window. Two girls. One was taller, with a helmet on. The other had pigtails and stuck her nose between the bars. Happy realized they were the daughters Diane had mentioned back at Shoemaker Stables.

"Be careful, Ivy," the taller one scolded. "He could bite."

"Oh, I don't think he'd do that," Diane reassured them.

Happy was relieved. He didn't want these people thinking he would ever bite anything other than hay, grain, and grass. And alfalfa. And clover, of course. And he loved the occasional apple or carrot for a treat. But he would never bite a person! It wasn't nice, and he could just tell that they wouldn't taste very good.

Then the shorter girl, Ivy, held out her

hand. "Come here, boy," she said. Her voice was quieter now. "It's okay. I won't hurt you."

Happy looked at the young girl's face. Even in the darkness of the stall, he could see that Ivy's eyes were soft and understanding. He took a step forward.

"What's his name again?" Andrea, the taller girl, asked.

Happy paused, wanting to hear what Diane would say.

"Happy Go Lucky is his show name. I think we'll just call him Happy around the barn," Diane said.

Happy was relieved that Diane got his name right. He looked at Ivy's hand again and moved another step closer.

"Yes, the name Happy will do nicely," Diane continued. "He needs a lot of practice before he'll be ready for shows, anyway. He has only had one rider so far."

"Wow," the taller girl said with a laugh. "He'll have a lot to learn."

Happy was just about to reach out to Ivy's hand, but the tone of the other girl's voice stopped him. What did she mean, he had a lot to learn? That wasn't fair! Happy took a step away from the people and dropped his head. He suddenly had a very bad feeling about this place. It didn't seem like the kind of place that should be called Big Apple Barn at all.

Ivy gave him one last look and pulled her hand away. "He's a beautiful pony, but he acts like he doesn't want to be here. I don't think the name Happy fits him very well."

"Oh, Ivy," Diane said with a sigh. "Let's not give up on him yet." Then the two girls followed their mother away, and Happy was left alone in his new home.

Chapter Five

The Visitor

Happy was miserable. He went to sleep as soon as Diane and her daughters left the barn. And why shouldn't he? There was nothing else for him to do. At Mrs. Shoemaker's he could leave his stall whenever he wanted, but not here. And all he could see when he looked out his window was the long row of horse stalls. That only made him more lonely for Gracie, his mother.

The next morning, Happy woke to a strange scratching noise. Either there was something with him in the stall, or his stall was haunted!

Happy pricked his ears and looked around. The stall had four walls, built with wooden planks. It was filled with straw, and there was a window that looked out into the aisle. The door had a top and bottom. When the top was open, Happy could put his head out. But the door was closed all the way now, and Happy appeared to be alone. He could still hear a scritchy-scratchy sound, though.

"Oh, you're awake," a voice squeaked. "You didn't touch your dinner. If you don't like grain, I can help you eat it."

Happy could hear someone, but he couldn't see a single soul!

"Unless you're sick," the squeaking

continued. "I don't want to eat after you if you are sick. Of course, it's not like mice and horses get the same illnesses, but I like to play it safe."

A mouse? That explained it! Happy lowered his head and took another look around. Sure enough, a tiny gray mouse was sitting in his feed bucket. The mouse held an enormous kernel of corn in his paws and stared at Happy with wide, black eyes.

"So, are you sick?"

Happy wasn't really sick, just heartsick, and being heartsick was hardly contagious. His stomach *was* empty. He was hungry enough to eat all of his feed and more, but he didn't know how he could say no to the mouse.

"I'm fine," Happy replied. "Go ahead and eat."

"So, you're new," the mouse said between bites. "I'm Roscoe." The mouse's cheeks were so full, Happy couldn't believe he could still talk.

"I'm Happy," the pony said.

"Not from around here?"

"I don't think so," Happy answered. He had no idea how far away Mrs. Shoemaker's barn was, but it felt like another world.

"Haven't lived in a barn like this before, have you?" Roscoe asked. His whiskers jiggled as he spoke, but he didn't take his eyes off Happy. "I'm just guessing, but you seem overwhelmed."

Happy nodded.

"Well, it's a good thing I'm here," the mouse said, poking himself in the chest. "I can tell you everything you need to know about this place."

Happy got the feeling that Roscoe had a lot to say.

"For starters, always look before you put your head in your feed bucket. I try not to fall asleep in the stalls, but sometimes I can't help it." Roscoe took another bite. "You should also be careful in the pasture. Making the right friends is important around here." Roscoe paused and even stopped chewing for a moment. He raised his eyebrows. Only when Happy nodded that he understood, did Roscoe take another bite.

"Of course, you'll always have me," Roscoe promised. "But horse friends are very different. Ms. Diane, she'll notice which horses you hang out with."

Happy nodded again.

"Prudence the cat thinks you'll be friends with Goldilocks," Roscoe said. "I'm not sure why she thinks that. I mean, she's never even met you. But Prudence has been the barn cat for a long time. She knows a lot, and she says Goldilocks will look after you."

Wait, Happy thought for a second. *Why is a mouse talking with a cat?* Sure, Happy was young, but he still knew that cats and mice were not usually friends. He questioned whether he could believe what Roscoe was saying. Either way, he'd have to remember the name Goldilocks. Just in case.

Just then, Happy heard footsteps coming down the barn aisle. It was Diane, and she was leading a caramel-colored pony and a tall, chestnut horse.

"Oh, it must be turn-out time," Roscoe

announced. "There's Goldi now. And Big Ben. I wonder if you'll get to go out in the pasture with them."

Happy watched, his eyes wide. Was Diane taking them out to a field? Just thinking about it, Happy got antsy. He needed to stretch his legs! Next, Andrea walked by with another horse. This one was a bold black, and he lifted his legs high as he

pranced along the aisle. The horse pulled forward, trying to drag Andrea along. But Andrea gave the lead rope a firm tug, and the horse slowed down.

"Oh, now that's Cobalt," Roscoe began. "You should keep an eye out for him —"

But before Roscoe could finish, Ivy's face appeared over the stall door.

"Good morning, Happy," Ivy said in a soft voice. "Do you want some grass? Mom said I can take you out to the field."

Happy tossed his head up and down. He pushed himself up against the door. He couldn't wait! Happy was so excited that he forgot all about his guest. He walked forward and let Ivy attach a lead to his halter.

"Thanks for the grain, Happy," Roscoe called. "I'll see you tomorrow."

Chapter Six

A Word of Advice

Happy looked over at Ivy. She barely came up to his chin, but Happy still trusted her. Ivy wore her hair in braids that bounced up and down as she walked. She gave him a little smile and scratched him behind his ear. Ivy must have known how much a pony liked to be scratched right there. Wearing a halter all the time could get itchy.

As they reached the end of the aisle, Happy was surprised to see that the sun was bright and bold. How long had he been in that dreary stall?

He looked ahead and gasped. He saw a wide green pasture that was almost as big as the one at Shoemaker Stables. It had three apple trees and lots of tall grass. The field was surrounded by a tall wooden fence.

There were already five horses and a pony inside. Happy felt his stomach growl, but he reminded himself not to rush. He walked right next to Ivy. His mom had taught him never to hurry ahead of someone leading him.

But as soon as Ivy opened the gate and took the rope off Happy's halter, the pony burst with excitement. He ran into the field and gave three hoof-kicking bucks right in a row. Once Happy reached the far fence, he turned around and headed straight back. It felt so good to be outside! He galloped two

full laps around the field. Just as he was about to buck again, he noticed Cobalt, the sleek black horse, watching him.

Cobalt was standing with three other young horses. The group nickered to one another as they pulled at tufts of grass. They had long legs and thick tails. Cobalt said something, and all four horses stopped eating and stared at Happy.

Happy looked around, feeling a little silly. Hadn't they ever seen a pony play before? Something told Happy they hadn't.

The horses murmured to one another, then Cobalt turned back toward Happy. "C'mere, kid."

Happy looked around again. Goldilocks and the handsome chestnut named Big Ben were the only other horses in the field, and they were busy eating. It made sense then, Happy realized, that the black horse was talking to him.

"Yeah, you," Cobalt said with a shake of his shiny mane. "The new guy."

Happy looked back at Goldi and Big Ben. He remembered what Roscoe had told him. Roscoe said that the barn cat thought Happy would be friends with Goldi. But Happy thought that Goldi and Big Ben looked much older than the other horses, and Happy wasn't sure he could just walk up to them. Happy wanted friends his own age. Besides, Goldi and Big Ben hadn't even bothered to say hello.

Happy stepped forward, trying to hold his nose up as he approached Cobalt and the horses. They were all much taller than he was. They were much taller than Gracie, too. It had been just him and his mother back at Shoemaker Stables. Happy had never talked to a horse before.

"What's your name?" the black horse asked.

"Happy." Happy looked up at the horse and thought he saw him smile, but if he did, it was only for a second.

"I'm Cobalt. This is Reggie," Cobalt said as he looked at a stocky gray horse. "And that is Max and Maurice." The other two horses were both dark brown, and they looked a lot alike.

"So, what brings you to Big Apple Barn? Did Diane tell you why you are here?" Cobalt asked.

Happy hesitated. "She said I am going to be a school pony," he answered. Happy tried to sound proud. He remembered what Mrs. Shoemaker and his mom had told him. His job would be very important.

"A school pony," Cobalt repeated. "Hear that, boys? The new guy, Happy, is a school pony." The horses all nodded. "Listen, kid, we've been here a while," Cobalt said, lowering his voice. "And we've all been

school horses, so let me give you some advice."

Happy stepped forward. That was nice of Cobalt. He needed advice. Diane had come to pick him up before his mother had been able to tell him much about his new home. He would be grateful for someone to tell him how things worked at Big Apple Barn.

"I bet they'll put Andrea on you, to try you out," Cobalt said, his voice a whisper. "You know her. She's the oldest daughter."

Happy nodded his head. Then Cobalt took a step forward, so his head was close to Happy's ear. "No matter what," Cobalt continued, "don't do what she asks you to. She's a good rider, but she and Diane will be hard on you if you go soft the first time. If you want to have an easier life here, you have to show them who is boss."

"Go soft?" Happy asked, trying to figure out what Cobalt was saying.

"You know, if you go soft, you're being too good," the dark horse explained. "You're making it too easy for the rider."

Happy gave Cobalt a long look. He could tell that the horse was smart. "Thanks, Cobalt," he replied. "That's good advice." He watched as the horses all went back to eating.

Happy really wanted to run some more. He still had so much energy! But Cobalt had been nice to him, and he didn't want to look rude by playing around. So Happy dropped his head and bit off a chunk of grass near the horses. It was almost as sweet as the grass back at Mrs. Shoemaker's place, but Happy wasn't thinking about that. He had other things on his mind.

Chapter Seven

Getting Ready

The next morning, Happy woke up to the sound of many horses whinnying. He had never heard anything like it. He must have slept through it the previous morning. But how? It was so noisy! Some of the horses' voices were high and playful while others were deep and dignified. They were all excited. It was feeding time.

Looking out his stall window, Happy could see Diane coming down the aisle with a wheelbarrow. Happy had seen Mrs. Shoemaker use a wheelbarrow in her garden before, but Diane's wheelbarrow was full of grain!

Happy scraped his front hoof against the ground as Diane neared his stall. He felt like he had never been so hungry in his life!

"Good morning, Happy!" Diane said as she came up to his stall door. "You look chipper today. Andrea will be here soon, and we'll get her to tack you up."

Happy knew what that meant. Andrea would put a saddle on his back and a bridle around his head. And then she would take him for a ride.

Diane smiled as she poured out a scoop of grain. Happy looked in his feed bucket to make sure Roscoe was not there. Then he plunged his head into the grain. *Yum.*

As he ate, Happy thought about what

Cobalt had said the day before. The sleek, black horse had been right. Andrea would be the first person to ride him at Big Apple Barn. If Cobalt knew that, his other advice was probably right, too.

Happy would have to show Diane and Andrea that he was the boss. Happy wanted to be a good school pony, but he was still young. He wanted to have some fun, too. He didn't want Diane to work him *too* hard.

After Happy finished his grain, he started to pace in his stall. He wished he had run more when he was out in the field yesterday. His legs felt bouncy. He needed to give them a good stretch. Why did he spend yesterday afternoon eating grass instead of running in the field? Happy wasn't used to being in a stall all of the time. At Shoemaker Stables, he could run and play whenever he wanted.

It wasn't too long before Andrea appeared

at Happy's door. "Hey, Happy," she greeted him. "Are you ready for a ride?"

Happy was ready. At least, he thought he was. He needed to be out of his stall, but he was a little worried about Andrea riding him.

Andrea opened the door and took hold of Happy's halter. She led him out of the stall and stopped next to a set of chains, one on each side of the aisle. "These are cross ties, Happy," Andrea explained. "I'll hook the chains onto your halter, so you'll know to stand right here."

Happy watched as Andrea attached the chains to his halter. This was the first time he had ever been in cross ties. Mrs. Shoemaker had always just tacked him up in his stall.

"That's good," Andrea said. "I'll be right back."

Happy watched as Andrea walked away.

He stepped forward to see where she was going, but he was jerked back. The cross ties stopped him! He felt the chains strain against his halter. Now he was all alone, and he was afraid to move. Where did Andrea go?

It felt like he had been standing there forever before Andrea came back. When he

saw her, Happy nickered in relief. So he would be out of the chains soon. *Phew!*

Andrea carried a saddle in one arm and a bucket of brushes in the other.

Brushes! Happy had forgotten how much he loved to be brushed.

"I'm going to pick your hooves first," Andrea explained.

Happy knew that Andrea needed to pick his hooves — she would use a small metal tool to clean out his feet. But Happy didn't really like it. He had to lift his hooves one at a time and try to balance on only three legs. It made him a little nervous, especially with those pesky chains attached to his halter.

Andrea was fast and moved from leg to leg, picking out clods of dirt from every hoof. He hadn't even liked it when Mrs. Shoemaker picked his hooves, and Andrea was practically a stranger.

He watched as Andrea dropped the hoof pick into the bucket and reached for a brush. Happy would let her pick his hooves all over again, as long as she gave him a good brushing.

"You look pretty clean," Andrea said, "so I'll just get the dust off." With swift, stiff motions, Andrea whisked the brush over Happy's back and legs. He could hardly even feel it! Mrs. Shoemaker would never have brushed him like that. Some horses might not like to be brushed, but Happy loved it — the harder the better.

Andrea barely touched his coat with the brush and Happy could still feel the itch of dirt close to his skin.

Then Andrea plopped the saddle on his back. Happy tossed his head in surprise, but the chains snapped at his halter. He didn't like the cross ties, and he didn't like having the saddle slammed on his back like that. Happy stamped his foot.

"Calm down, Happy. It's just a saddle," Andrea scolded. Then she reached around for the girth. It would go under Happy's belly and hold the saddle in place.

As Andrea buckled the girth, Happy flinched. It felt too tight! He put his ears back and stamped his foot again.

"Oh, it's not so bad, is it?" Andrea said, now holding the bridle. She put the reins over Happy's head and unhooked his halter.

This was all happening so fast. Before Happy knew it, the cold bit was in his mouth, and Andrea was fastening the bridle in place. Just like that, he was ready for his first ride at Big Apple Barn.

But suddenly he didn't feel ready. His saddle felt like it didn't fit. Was there a fold in the saddle pad, or dirt on his back?

Something wasn't right. And he was sure his girth was too tight. Happy put his ears back again, hoping Andrea would help him.

"Let's go to the outside ring," Andrea said.

She walked ahead and pulled on the reins. Happy followed reluctantly.

Once he was out of the barn, Happy stopped worrying about his saddle. His legs were bouncy again and he needed to run. It was all he could think about.

"There's our new pony," Diane said, smiling. She and Ivy sat on the fence next to the riding ring. The ring was much bigger than the one at Shoemaker Stables. There was plenty of room for a pony with lots of energy.

"Yep, here he is," Andrea replied. "Do you want me to get on?"

"Sure," Diane said. "Let's see what he's made of."

With a swing of her leg, Andrea was on Happy's back, putting her weight in the saddle stirrups and shortening the reins. She first made a clicking sound with her tongue, then gave Happy a light nudge with her heel. And Happy took off at full speed.

Chapter Eight

A Hard Gallop

"Whoa!" Andrea yelled, pulling at the reins with all her strength.

But Happy wasn't paying attention to Andrea. He only wanted to run. His legs galloped beneath him, pounding against the sandy ground. They took him faster and faster around the ring.

Happy knew he should stop, but it felt so good to stretch his legs. It took his mind off the painful saddle and the too-tight girth. If he ran, he didn't have to think about how things used to be at Shoemaker Stables. If he could just keep running, maybe he wouldn't have to worry about all the new things in his life at Big Apple Barn.

Happy knew he was being bad. Andrea had not asked him to run. She had only asked him to walk. But Happy needed to run, and he couldn't stop himself.

All at once, Cobalt's words of advice flashed through his head. Happy had not wanted to disobey. He had only wanted to show Diane and Andrea that he could be a good school pony if he had a good rider. But it was too late for that.

At last, Happy started to feel tired. His breath was short, and his legs began to slow down. "Steady, boy," Andrea said.

Pulling lightly on one of the reins, she asked him to run in smaller circles. Happy listened to her and turned.

"That's good, Andrea," Diane called. "Let him work through it."

Now that Happy had released some of his extra energy, he could concentrate on Andrea's requests. He could tell that Andrea was a good rider, and he felt bad for running off with her on his back. It wasn't what Mrs. Shoemaker or Happy's mom would have wanted him to do at all.

"Okay, Andrea," Diane said, scooting off the fence. "I think he's done enough."

Andrea pulled Happy to a stop and gave him a halfhearted pat on his neck.

Diane walked over as Andrea climbed down. Ivy followed a few steps behind her mother. The younger daughter looked at Happy with sad eyes.

"He was good once he calmed down," Andrea said. "But I don't think he's ready to be a real school pony. He needs too good of a rider."

Diane looked at Andrea and gave her a small nod. Then she turned toward Happy. "Well," she replied, her voice quiet, "I must say I am disappointed. I had hoped he would be ready to be a school pony. He seemed so sweet at Mrs. Shoemaker's."

"I think it's going to take a while," Andrea said matter-of-factly.

Happy looked from Andrea to Diane, and then to Ivy. They all looked disappointed. Happy felt disappointed, too.

Ivy had offered to bring Happy back to his stall. He was hot and sweaty, and she had to walk him for a long time to cool him down.

Then she gave him a good, long brushing, just the way Happy liked. She rubbed his tired back and legs with a soft rag.

It was so comforting to have someone take care of him, but Happy felt awful. He had not been a good pony at all, so why was Ivy being so nice to him?

"Oh, Happy," Ivy said with a sigh. "It must be hard to move to a new place. I hope you start to like it better here." She reached around his neck and gave him a light hug. "Get some rest," she suggested. Then she let herself out of the stall.

Before her kind words could sink in, Happy heard another voice — a much higher voice.

"You showed them, didn't you?" It was Roscoe. The little mouse was perched at the back of Happy's stall. He was sitting in a hole in the wall that was just a little lower than Happy's eye level, and he was shaking his head.

"What do you mean?" Happy asked, stepping toward his visitor.

"You proved that you were the boss," Roscoe replied. As he spoke, he reached up and cleaned his whiskers.

"I couldn't really help it," Happy tried to explain. "Those cross ties made me nervous, and then my girth was too tight." Even as he spoke, Happy knew his excuses sounded like just that . . . excuses. "Besides," he continued, "Cobalt told me to do that. He told me to show Andrea who was boss."

Roscoe just shook his head. "I know what Cobalt told you. He was bragging about it earlier," the mouse said. "I tried to tell you to watch out for Cobalt. He's not bad. It's just that he's not much older than we are. He doesn't know everything."

Roscoe spoke so fast, Happy had a hard time taking everything in.

"Prudence the cat says that Cobalt doesn't know how to work with people yet. You could have really messed things up today."

Happy dropped his head. It was bad enough having Diane, Andrea, and Ivy be disappointed with him, but the barn mouse, too? "I know," Happy agreed. "I didn't *want* to be bad. It just kind of happened."

"The good news is that it's not too late. So, listen up," Roscoe said, tugging at his own ear. "Prudence always says: 'Don't try to impress anyone but yourself.'"

Happy rolled his eyes. Was he really going to take advice from a mouse? A mouse that took advice from a barn cat? Besides, where was this Prudence the cat?

Happy was about to ask, but then he heard a rustling noise. "What was that?"

"Oh, it's just Big Ben," Roscoe said, pointing to the hole behind him. "Diane is riding him in the indoor ring. That's where all the big jumps are. Wanna see?" Just then, Roscoe jumped from the hole in the wall, and landed right on Happy's nose. Then he scrambled up Happy's face and sat down

between his ears. "If you look through the hole, you can see into the indoor ring."

Happy did as Roscoe said, lowering his head so he could look through the gap in the wall. Sure enough, Happy could see the tall, regal chestnut horse trotting in a large ring. It looked just like the ring outside, but it was under a tall roof.

"You're lucky," Roscoe said. "The horse that was in this stall before kicked a hole through the wall. So you've got a great view."

Happy gave a slight nod, but he wasn't listening to Roscoe. He was too busy watching Big Ben. The horse looked so strong and graceful, carrying Diane on his back. They seemed like such a team. Big Ben was cantering now, which was faster than a trot. He sped up when Diane nudged him with her leg, and he slowed down when she squeezed the reins.

"Prudence says that Big Ben is the top horse in the barn," Roscoe said. This time, Happy didn't question Roscoe or Prudence. This horse was clearly one of the best.

Happy was watching as Big Ben headed toward a tall fence in the middle of the ring. Happy held his breath. The fence was very high, but Ben and Diane sailed right over it.

"Wow," Happy breathed.

"Yeah, I know," Roscoe said.

Happy and Roscoe watched until Diane pulled Big Ben to a halt. She brought him to the center of the ring. Then both Diane and Andrea, who had been looking on, gave the tall horse long, hearty pats.

"Now *that's* a horse that knows how to work with people," Roscoe said.

Happy nodded again, and this time he heard just what Roscoe was saying.

Chapter Nine

A Second Chance

By the next day, Happy had had a lot of time to think about things. What he needed was a second chance. He hoped he would get it.

He was glad to see Diane stop in front of his stall that morning. She held a lead rope in one hand. "I know you got a good run yesterday, Happy," she said, "but I bet you'd like to get out of your stall again today."

Happy rushed toward the door. If Andrea wanted to ride him again, he would be much better. He knew he could be.

But Happy's spirits changed when he realized Diane was only taking him out to the field. He wasn't sure he wanted to go into the pasture again. That's where all the trouble had started. Happy dragged his hooves as he walked through the gate, stirring up a cloud of dust.

When he looked around the field, he saw the exact same horses who had been there his first time. Happy couldn't believe it. There was a whole barn full of horses, and he was turned out with Big Ben, Goldi, Cobalt, and all the young horse's friends again.

Happy didn't feel like running today. He didn't really feel like eating grass, either. He had decided he would stand by himself in a corner of the field, when he noticed Cobalt walking up to him. The dark horse's friends were all trailing behind.

"Hey there, Happy," Cobalt said, swishing his tail.

"Hey, Cobalt," Happy replied cautiously.

"So you showed Andrea and Diane that they have to respect you," Cobalt said. "Nice work. I don't think you'll have to worry about being worked too hard now."

Happy didn't know what to say. He felt like he still had plenty to worry about.

"I was used all the time for riding lessons when I first got here," Cobalt continued. "But now I only have to do one or two classes a week. Only the best riders can stay on me."

Happy nodded. It sounded like Cobalt didn't like to be ridden very much. That was fine for Cobalt, but Happy actually *did* like to be ridden. He didn't want to work all the time, but, the more he thought about it, he liked the idea of having lots of kids ride him. He wanted to show Andrea — and Diane especially — that he could be a good school pony.

"I'm glad things worked out for you, Cobalt," Happy said. He realized then that Cobalt hadn't tried to give Happy bad advice. Cobalt just wanted different things than Happy did.

Cobalt and his friends started eating grass next to Happy. Happy still wasn't that hungry until a fresh, sweet scent hit his nose. It smelled so familiar, but where was it coming from? Happy's nose twitched, full of the smell.

"Is there clover around here?" Happy asked, searching the field.

Cobalt lifted his head. "Oh, sure," Cobalt replied. "It's over where Big Ben and Goldi are standing. They always graze there."

Happy was so excited. Clover! Just like at Shoemaker Stables!

But then he paused. Goldi and Big Ben were already there. It was their patch of clover. Besides, they had most likely heard all about how he had run off with Andrea the day before. If Big Ben was really the best horse in the barn, he most likely wouldn't approve of what Happy had done.

The wind carried the honeyed scent of clover over to Happy's corner of the pasture again. He couldn't resist. It smelled too good.

"I'll see you guys later," Happy said with a nod to Cobalt. Then he headed toward the clover patch where the tall, chestnut horse and the caramel-colored pony stood.

Happy hesitated as he approached Big Ben and Goldie. They were busy chomping on clover. Happy's mouth began to water. How could he, the new pony, just come up and start eating next to these two well-respected horses? He took another step

toward the clover patch and paused, his ears pricked forward.

Goldi lifted her head and looked right at Happy. She chewed slowly and then swallowed. "Well, Big Ben," Goldi said, nudging the horse next to her. "Look who has finally come over to see us."

Big Ben raised his head, too. When he had stopped chewing, he said, "Indeed. We have company. Welcome, Happy Go Lucky."

How did they know his name? And his full name at that! Happy was suddenly even more anxious than before. *I should just turn around and forget about the clover*, he thought. He took a step back.

Then Goldi turned toward Happy. "We knew you would come over sooner or later," she said, her voice even and kind. "Your mother, Gracie, had a sweet tooth for clover, too."

Chapter Ten

A Big Apple

Happy looked from Big Ben to Goldi, not knowing what to say. Was it true? Did they know his mom?

"We were your mother's best friends when she lived at Big Apple Barn," Goldi explained, sensing his confusion.

"It isn't the same without her here," Big Ben said. "She was always the best at discovering new patches of clover," he added with a chuckle.

Happy couldn't believe it! His mom had actually lived here. Now he knew why she was so sure that Big Apple Barn would be a good home for him. At least it would have been, if he hadn't messed everything up.

"Diane had been talking about how you were coming," Goldi explained. "She's excited to have you here. Gracie was one of her best school ponies ever, and good new school ponies aren't easy to find."

Happy kicked at the grass. "I'm not so sure she's glad to have me now," he said. "I wasn't very good yesterday." He didn't know how much else he should say. He looked at Goldi and Big Ben again, and he saw understanding in their eyes. "I bolted with Andrea on my back," Happy said quickly. "I was so nervous, and I had so much energy. I just couldn't stop." Happy lowered his head, expecting to be scolded.

"Happy," Goldi soothed him. "It was your first time being ridden in a new place. It takes time to get used to new things. Diane understands. She's worked with lots of new ponies and horses."

Happy looked up again, hopeful.

Big Ben simply nodded his noble head.

"Don't worry yourself over it, Happy," Goldi advised. "Things will work out."

Happy sighed with relief. He looked at Goldi, and he wanted to believe her.

"In the meantime, help yourself to some clover," the older pony offered.

Happy had almost forgotten about the clover! He reached down and nibbled a few tender buds. They tasted so good! Almost like home! After a few more bites, Happy felt a surge of joy. He wasn't so alone here after all. Goldi and Big Ben knew Gracie, his mom. And there was lots of clover.

A bright butterfly flitted by. Happy said good-bye to Goldi and Big Ben, then trotted after the butterfly. He felt so good, he gave a playful buck and almost forgot he was in a new place.

Then he heard his name. "Happy!"

He looked around.

It was Diane, Andrea, and Ivy. They were all standing by the pasture fence, and they were watching him.

He ran toward the gate.

"What do you think?" Diane asked her daughters. "Should we give him another try?"

Happy tossed his head, hoping for his second chance.

They brought him in from the field, and they all worked to give him a good brushing. They combed his mane and tail and took the brush over his whole body.

Happy savored every second. He felt good and clean, even after the saddle was on his back. When it was time for Andrea to buckle the girth, he didn't pin back his ears. And this time, the girth didn't feel too tight.

Andrea led Happy outside. Diane and Ivy climbed onto the fence by the ring, so they could watch. Happy stood still as Andrea pulled herself into the saddle. He waited for her to tell him what to do. He listened very closely. He didn't want to mess up again.

He thought about everything Mrs. Shoemaker had taught him, and he remembered his mother's best advice about how a pony and rider work together. Now he knew she had learned that lesson during her days as a school pony at Big Apple Barn.

Happy was nervous, but he walked, trotted, and cantered on cue. He even

hopped over the small jump in the center of the ring. Andrea was a good rider. She knew how to tell Happy what she wanted, and Happy could do what she asked if he paid attention.

When Andrea eventually pulled Happy to a halt, he was breathing heavily. It was hard work being good! Diane and Ivy clapped. Then they hurried over to Happy's side and gave him a long pat.

"He was so good!" Andrea exclaimed. "He

did everything just like I told him. It seemed like he really wanted to work with me."

"That sounds like the sign of a good school pony," Diane said. "Just like his mom."

Ivy didn't say anything. She simply scratched him behind his ears. Diane and her daughters walked with Happy as he cooled down. Then they took him back to the barn, removed his saddle and bridle, and took him to his stall.

As Happy stepped into the stall, he saw Roscoe sitting on the rim of his feed bucket. The mouse gave him a thumbs-up sign and a toothy grin.

Happy reached down and brushed his nose to the mouse's pink ears. "Thanks," he whispered.

Then Happy whirled around and put his head over his stall door. Diane, Andrea, and Ivy were still there, waiting for him.

"Look at Happy now, Mom," Andrea said. "I think he likes being here."

"I hope he does," Diane replied. "I like having him, and I'm sure our riding students will, too."

Happy tossed his head up and down and gave a lively whinny.

"You know what?" Ivy said in her soft voice. "I think Happy is a really good name for him, after all."

"You're right, Ivy," Diane agreed. "Happy fits him perfectly."

Happy couldn't have agreed more.

Diane and Andrea turned to walk down the aisle, but Ivy stayed with Happy.

"Here you go, boy," Ivy said. "You were such a good pony today." In her hand, she held the biggest, juiciest apple Happy had ever seen!

Carefully, Happy bit into the apple. It was

so big he couldn't get his mouth all of the way around it! He reached out for the rest of the apple, then licked the juice from Ivy's hand. Ivy giggled.

As Happy tasted the sweetness of the apple, he looked from Roscoe to Ivy. And he thought of Diane and Andrea, Goldi and Big Ben. That's when he decided that Big Apple Barn was a good name for this place, too. It was big and new, but he had found friends. And he was sure he would have a lot of adventures here. But most of all, Big Apple Barn felt like a happy home. And Happy felt like a lucky pony.

What Makes a Pony a Pony?

A pony is a pony because of its size, not its age. In general, horses under a certain size are ponies. That size is 58 inches.

While size is the main part of being a pony, there is more to it. A pony's legs are usually shorter in relation to its body than a horse's legs. And ponies are usually stockier than horses, with shorter backs. Many also say that being a pony is about personality! Ponies often seem to have different personalities than horses. For the most part, ponies are smart, hardy, reliable, and sure-footed. Each one is distinct, but they are all true characters!

Glossary

Pieces of Tack

When you put the riding gear on a horse, it is called "tacking up." The different pieces of equipment together are called the "tack."

Bit — The bit is the piece of the bridle that goes in the horse or pony's mouth. It is attached to the reins and helps the pony understand the rider's directions.

Bridle — The bridle goes on the pony's head. It includes the bit and the reins.

Girth — The girth is a piece of leather or fabric that goes under the pony's belly to connect one side of the saddle to the other. If pulled tight, it keeps the saddle in place.

Lead rope — A lead rope is a long rope with a clip on the end. The rider can clip it to a loop on the pony's halter to lead the pony.

Reins — The reins are part of the bridle. They connect the bit and the rider's hands. With the reins, the rider can steer and tell a pony to slow down or stop.

Saddle — The saddle goes on the pony's back, and the rider sits on it. It is usually made of leather and helps a rider stay on.

Saddle Pad — The saddle pad goes on the pony's back, under the saddle. It helps keep the saddle from rubbing against the horse.

Stirrups — The stirrups are part of the saddle. They are metal rings that hang from each side of the saddle and provide support for a rider's foot.

Wraps — There are many kinds of leg wraps for horses and ponies. Wraps protect a pony's legs during travel or exercise.

About the Author

Kristin Earhart grew up in Worthington, Ohio, where she spent countless waking and sleeping hours dreaming about horses and ponies. She started riding lessons at eight, and her trainer really was named Diane, and Diane really did know a lot about ponies. Kristin's pony, Moochie, and her horse, Wendy, were two of the best friends a girl could have. So is her husband, with whom she lives in Brooklyn, New York.